The Amazing Team of Kids

A. Marino

Cover art and Illustrations by

Vico Coceres

ISBN:
9781711799193

DEDICATION

To my cousins E., I., C. and T., and my Uncles Jeff and Will.

CONTENTS

ACKNOWLEDGMENTS

Thanks to my Mom and Dad and my little brother

CHAPTER ONE

SUPERHERO TRAINING

Johnny was anxious as they walked out of the airport.

"Don't worry, Johnny", said his mother. "You will make good friends at your new school."

Johnny opened the car door and said, "Mom, I wish we were back in California."

"Honey, you will be all right," said his mom as she started the engine.

Johnny had just moved to Baltimore, Maryland with his mom for her new job. He was a tall, handsome boy with straight, brown hair. He wore black shoes and really liked the color blue. He wore blue clothes almost every day.

When they got to the new apartment Johnny looked around and said, "This is a nice place."

The apartment was small, but had tall ceilings and nice furniture. There was lots of sunlight coming in through the windows. There were pink chairs around a white table in the dining room. Under the table there was a blue carpet with white polka dots. The kitchen cabinets were painted white, and the walls were painted blue and turquoise. There was also a white couch against the wall in the living room with a large TV in front of it. There was a fancy bathroom right next to the living room. When Johnny entered his bedroom, he saw that his bed had blue sheets, a blue blanket, and blue pillow cases.

Tired from all the travel, Johnny went to bed early. During the night, Johnny tossed and turned in his bed. He was having a nightmare. He dreamt he was being chased by a wicked villain. He was all black with red eyes. He woke up terrified.

In the morning, Johnny's mother tried to make him feel better by letting him eat his favorite cereal, Superhero Flakes. Superhero Flakes were corn flakes shaped like tiny super heroes. They were covered in sugar and were colored blue.

As he ate his breakfast, Johnny could not stop worrying about his first day of high school.

"Mom, I'm really nervous about my first day," said Johnny.

"Honey, you will be making lots of good friends at your new school, so stop worrying, dear," Johnny's mom said. "You might even see some of your old friends."

"Well, I really hope nobody bothers me today," Johnny mumbled.

Suddenly, the school bus pulled up in front of his apartment.

"Honey, you should go," said his mom, handing him his backpack.

Johnny put on his shoes and rushed out of the apartment. His mother leaned out of the window.

"Good luck!" said his mother as he stepped onto the school bus.

On the bus, he did not see anyone he recognized. He sat by himself. The bus arrived at school and Johnny walked into the building, not even looking to see what his new school looked like.

When Johnny got to his locker, he opened it and was surprised to see a portal spinning 'round and 'round. Johnny was so amazed that he touched the portal with the tip of his finger. Suddenly, he found himself standing in front of a tall skyscraper, labeled "Superhero Training". Then, he saw one of his old friends from middle school walk out of the building. His name was Diego.

Diego was a tall, skinny teenager with black, curly hair. He was wearing a red shirt and shorts.

"Hi Diego," he said. "Do you know where we are?"

"Welcome to Superhero Training, Johnny," Diego said.

"Yeah, but where exactly am I?" asked Johnny. "I have to get back to high school before I'm late for class. Otherwise, I'll get detention."

"Me too," said Diego. "Come on, let me show you inside."

"This is a nightmare," moaned Johnny.

Inside he saw some other old friends from middle school, Brian and Luciana. Brian was a tall boy with brown hair and brown eyes. He had a blue shirt on and a pair of green shorts. Luciana was a small girl with golden blonde hair. She had hazel eyes. She wore a pink t-shirt and a pair of turquoise shorts.

"Come on," said Brian. "We have to do our Superhero Training."

"Alright," said Johnny, "But this really is a nightmare."

"First things first," said Diego. "We have to make robot lookalikes of ourselves and send them to high school so people don't realize we are gone!"

"But we won't learn anything," complained Johnny.

Before anyone could respond, Luciana clapped her hands twice, and four robots that looked exactly like them started marching out the door.

"They will get detention instead," said Luciana.

"I'll get us a trainer," said Brian as he ran up to one of the lady trainers.

Several trainers came and said, "We need to see what powers each of you have." Each trainer took a kid by the hand. One lady trainer took Johnny by the hand and they walked into a big room with no furniture.

"Now close your eyes and imagine your happiest memory," said the trainer.

Johnny did as he was told. When he opened his eyes, Johnny saw the room covered with ice! Snowflakes were falling down from the ceiling.

"So, what powers do I have?" asked Johnny.

"Ice and snow," said the trainer. "Now let's go check on your friends."

As they walked down the hallway, Johnny passed a room with burning flames and fire inside. In the middle of the fire he saw Diego standing with his eyes closed.

"So, Diego has fire?!" Johnny asked the trainer.

"Yep!" answered the trainer.

They walked down the hall even further until they reached another room. Inside the room there were lightning bolts striking up and down. In the middle of the room Brian was standing with a smile on his face as he saw his powers.

"This is amazing!" shouted Brian to the trainer.

Johnny and the trainer walked even farther down to the last room of the hallway.

Inside, there was water splashing everywhere and a flood flowing inside. Luciana stood in the middle of the room.

The trainer said, "I think we should help clean up the mess you guys made with your powers."

They put a heater in the room that Johnny had filled with ice, sprayed water on the fire in Diego's room, and covered up the holes from the lightning bolts in Brian's room.

They were about to open the door in Luciana's room to help clean up the water when Luciana said, "I got this, guys!" Luciana reached out her hands and sucked up all the water.

Soon the rooms were spic and span, clean as before.

"Hey guys! Guess what my powers are?" asked Brian. "I get lightening!"

"I get to control water and can go underwater and breath air!" said Luciana

"Wait till you see my powers!" exclaimed Diego as a flame flew out of his hand.

"Let me guess," answered Luciana. "Fire."

"All this superhero work is exhausting. When are we going to have a break?" asked Diego.

"Right now," said the trainer.

CHAPTER TWO

DISAPPEARED!

"For break time, you can go to the library and study how to control your powers, or you can go up to homeroom and play some video games," said the trainer.

"Yay!" shouted Brian, Johnny, and Diego at the same time as they rushed upstairs.

"I'll study," said Luciana as she marched to the library.

An hour later, Johnny, Diego, and Brian were playing the Super Mario Brothers video game.

"When will you ever stop?" asked Luciana as she sat in a cozy corner of the room.

Suddenly, an announcement boomed on the loudspeaker, "All first-year students report to room Y for your next lesson."

"That's us," said Luciana.

Johnny and his friends rushed down the hallway and stopped in front of a room labeled "Room Y". Just then, a crowd of first years all lined up behind them. Then, a trainer stepped out of the classroom and said, "Everybody come inside!"

Everybody rushed inside and sat at a random desk.

"Now we will take attendance," said the trainer.

After they had taken attendance, a bunch of trainers came in, and each took one kid by the hand and led them to a training room.

One trainer took Johnny by the hand and led him into a purple training room. In the middle of the room was a large pot.

"Now," said the trainer, "Shoot with your powers at the pot."

Johnny did as he was told. Then the trainer clapped her hands three times and 5000 pots magically appeared right in front of Johnny.

"Now shoot at all of these within one minute," said the trainer. Johnny was only able to shoot 100 pots.

"Point your hands at the rest of the pots, close your eyes, and shoot!" shouted the trainer.

When Johnny opened his eyes, he saw that the rest of the pots were frozen solid.

"Now, I am going to put a robot with a water gun right in front of you. If you are able to freeze him in time, you will pass the test. If he is able to squirt water at you first, then you have not passed the test," said the trainer.

The trainer clapped her hands. A robot appeared right in front of Johnny with a water gun, ready to squirt. Johnny held his breath as he pointed his hands right at the robot. He had frozen the robot and passed the test!

"Great work. I want you to complete this by tomorrow," said the trainer as she handed him his homework.

Back in homeroom, Johnny was giddy with excitement. "I passed the test!" yelled Johnny.

"Me too!" yelled Diego.

"I did, too!" shouted Luciana.

"So did I!" exclaimed Brian.

In order to get home at the end of the day, Johnny walked to a secret elevator at the entrance of the building. The secret elevator had golden walls and silver buttons. He typed in his street name. Johnny clutched a golden bar on the wall as the elevator began to move swiftly. Suddenly, the elevator doors opened and he was standing right in front of his apartment!

Johnny walked out of the elevator. The elevator doors closed and vanished.

The next morning, Johnny's mother made eggs, bacon, and toast. Johnny wolfed down his breakfast.

"Johnny, don't eat your breakfast so fast. You might choke!" said his mother.

"I'm just so hungry!" said Johnny, as he rushed out the door to catch the bus.

Later, when Johnny got to school, he opened his locker, put away his things, and hopped into the portal. At first, he felt himself spinning in the air. Then, the portal stopped spinning, and he landed right in front of Superhero Training High School.

An announcement on the loudspeaker said, "All first-years please report to Room N." Johnny rushed inside and lined up in front of Room N.

"Please come in," said the trainer.

Once they were all in, the teacher said, "Pick another student to be your partner."

Diego and Brian picked each other, so Johnny picked Luciana.

"Now," said the teacher, "One of the trainers in the back will take you to the training rooms so they can teach you how to fly."

After the instructions were given, one trainer went with Luciana and Johnny to a training room.

The trainer said, "Close your eyes and imagine that you are flying high in the sky."

Luciana and Johnny did as they were told. When they opened their eyes, they were up in the air, flying.

"Whoa!" cried Johnny.

"Amazing, right?!" asked Luciana.

"Do a double loop," ordered the trainer.

"How do I do that?" asked Johnny.

"Just imagine yourself swooping down and doing a loop," said the trainer.

Johnny did a perfect double loop.

"How do I steer?" asked Johnny.

"To steer, lean right if you want to go right. Lean left if you want to go left. To go forward, lean forward."

"What about going up and down?" asked Johnny.

"Look up to go up, and look down to go down," answered the trainer.

"Oh, now I get it," said Luciana as she flew upwards.

"Practice over the weekend, because we are going to have a flying test next Monday," said the trainer.

"Also, here is some more homework. It is due next Tuesday." She picked up some homework and handed it to them.

At the end of the day, Johnny used the secret elevator to get back to his apartment. He was surprised to see that his mother was not there.

His mother had left a note, saying: "Johnny, I am going to the supermarket. I'll come home at 6:00 PM." Johnny read the note, took out his homework, and started completing it. When he was done, he put it back in his backpack and decided to read a book.

Soon it was 6:00 PM. Johnny peeked at the door and sat there waiting for his mother to arrive. But his mother didn't come. Johnny waited on the couch until 6:30.

"What on Earth?" said Johnny. He put down his book and rushed out the door. He saw Luciana, Diego, and Brian walking toward him.

"What are you guys doing out here?" asked Johnny.

"We came to see if your mom was home," explained Brian.

"Well, she's not. She just disappeared!" said Johnny.

"Our moms too!" exclaimed Diego.

"Something's up guys," said Luciana.

"Hey guys, why don't we just try to call them on our cellphones?" suggested Diego.

Everyone tried to call their moms, but nobody answered.

"Now what?" asked Brian.

"Why don't you guys just stay at my apartment until our moms get back?" suggested Johnny.

The next morning, Johnny was sharing his Superhero Flakes with everyone. Suddenly the phone rang. Luciana answered it. After a few minutes she said, "Hey guys, it's Superhero Training. They want us to come over."

"For what?" asked Johnny.

"I don't know," said Luciana. "Maybe they know what happened to our moms. I'll send our robot lookalikes to school right now, she said as she clapped her hands twice.

26

When they got there, a woman with long, blonde hair greeted them. She was dressed in a red, velvet dress.

"Hi, my name is Dr Morgan. I am the head of Superhero Training," she said. "I believe I know where your moms are. I sense that they are with the Evil King."

"But what Evil King? Wh-where do we go to find them?" Diego stammered.

"I'm sorry, but that's all I can tell you," said Dr. Morgan.

And with one snap of her fingers, they were back in Johnny's apartment.

CHAPTER THREE

THE EVIL KING

The next day at home, Johnny was rummaging through his closet.

"Hey guys, over here!" Johnny shouted. His friends rushed over. "Look at this!"

Johnny pointed to a shiny, glowing, blue crystal.

"Well, let's see what happens when we touch it," said Diego.

"Are you crazy?" said Luciana "That thing could kill us!"

"There's only one way to find out," said Johnny, as his hand approached the glowing crystal.

When Johnny touched the glowing crystal, he felt himself falling through darkness. He finally landed on a grassy surface.

Johnny asked himself, "Where on Earth am I?"

He looked around. He was sitting on grass in the middle of a dark forest. The glowing crystal he just touched was hovering in the air next to him.

Just then, Luciana, Diego, and Brian came falling to the ground.

"What is this place?" asked Brian.

"It seems as though we are in a different dimension," replied Johnny.

The world was totally black. All the trees were black. There were no colors. They dusted themselves off and walked out of the forest into a city. They were standing in the middle of a street with black cars, black houses with black windows. There were tall, black skyscrapers that appeared to be torn up.

"Hello!' said a voice behind them. The kids whirled around and were surprised to see a black fox staring right at them.

"If you're a fox, shouldn't you be orange?" asked Brian.

"Orange?" asked the fox. "Well, yes, I used to be orange. If you are visitors here, you should know all about the Evil King."

"Evil King?" asked Diego, "That's who we need to see!"

The fox looked at Diego warily.

"Well, the Evil King is a very mean king. He is our king. We used to have lots of different colors, but then the king took them away. It was horrible. Now the whole kingdom is moody and sad. But the only way to break the king's curse is to find the key he hid, and unlock the magical cage. He also captured four moms from the human world. Nobody knows what he is going to do with them."

"Guys, we have to save them!" said Luciana.

"Now is not the time," said the fox. "Why don't you stay at my house until morning?"

"Sure," replied Johnny. They set off to the fox's home. Finally, they stopped in front of a big, dark cave with a black mat in front of it.

"This is my home," said the fox as he picked up a basket of black berries.

"Here," he said, handing the basket to Johnny. "That's all I have for dinner."

"Ok," said Johnny, as he and the others started stuffing handfuls of berries in their mouths.

When the kids finished eating their berries, they slept in the corners of the cave. In the morning, the kids set off to the tall skyscraper where the king lived.

When they got there, Brian asked, "What's this?" as he looked at a black button on the wall.

"Press it!" said Luciana.

Brian pressed it and the walls opened. They stepped inside and saw two black doors and a narrow black hallway. One of the doors was open and they tiptoed to it. They peeked inside. There was a massive room. In the middle of the room they saw all of their moms sitting locked in a cage.

"Help!" they cried.

"Be Quiet!" yelled the Evil King.

The Evil King was dressed all in black and had red eyes. The kids noticed the Evil King was distracted. They had to act quickly!

Brian shot a lightning bolt at the lock of the cage and the lock opened. Out came all the mothers, hugging their children and running toward the exit.

"Get back here!" roared the Evil King. He pointed in their direction. Hundreds of guards stepped out and raced towards them, their daggers raised high.

The four teens picked up their moms and flew out of the building. They flew toward the forest. Johnny found the blue crystal again, touched it, and they were all teleported back home.

CHAPTER FOUR

THE DISAPPEARING CLOTHES

The kids were continuing to work hard. They were still getting high grades in school and in Superhero Training. One day Johnny found the same glowing crystal in his closet.

He touched it again, but this time nothing happened.

"Weird," he said to himself. Then he noticed that his clothes in his closet were gone! The clothes he was wearing were gone too!

"What happened?" shouted Johnny.

Johnny borrowed his mom's clothes. He was wearing her jeans and her red shirt that said "Girl's Rule!" He grabbed his own hoodie to cover the shirt.

"Why are you wearing a hoodie?" asked Diego when Johnny got to school.

Johnny explained everything to him.

"Promise you won't tell anybody?" asked Johnny.

"I promise," said Diego.

The next day, Johnny discovered that his alarm clock was gone. And the day after that, he noticed his mom's jewelry was gone. His mom was not happy!

"What's going on?" Johnny asked himself.

The next day at school, an announcement came on the loudspeaker:

"All students! Duck, Cover, Hold!"

They peeked out the nearest window and saw a giant robot throwing Johnny's mom's jewelry and Johnny's clothes. The robot's roar was Johnny's alarm clock sound.

"Oh, so that's where everything went," said Johnny as he rushed under his desk.

"Guys, we should go out and fight. Remember, we are superheroes. That's our job!" said Luciana.

"Are you kidding, Luciana?" shouted Diego. "That thing will kill us!"

"But it's our job!" said Luciana. "Who's with me?"

"I am!" said Johnny.

"Me too!" said Brian. Everybody stared at Diego. There was a long silence. Then finally he whispered softly, "OK, fine. Let's go for it."

CHAPTER FIVE

THE GIANT ROBOT

"Excuse me," said Johnny to the teacher. "Some of us have to go to the lavatory."

"Be quick," said the teacher.

Johnny and the kids rushed out of the classroom and jumped out of the nearest window. They flew over to the gigantic robot.

Luciana, Brian, Diego, and Johnny used their powers against the evil robot's body.

Soon the robot broke down and fell to the ground. Out came the Evil King with a big, mega sized gun ready to shoot! Johnny froze him before he could shoot, and Luciana washed the broken robot and frozen Evil King away.

Lots of kids and teachers came out and started cheering and shouting for joy.

Then the kids flew back into a window in the hallway and rushed back to the classroom.

"What took you so long?" asked the teacher when they arrived.

"Sorry," said Diego. "We had to..."

"I don't want to hear about it," said the teacher.

After school Johnny went home. He ate a delicious salad and some chicken, and went to bed. In the middle of the night, Johnny looked at the starry nighttime sky and fell into a deep sleep, wondering what he would do tomorrow for Superhero Training.

Meanwhile, the Evil King's son, Prince Polo, wanted to get revenge on the kids for freezing his father. Prince Polo looked almost exactly like his dad, except he was slightly shorter and had glowing, yellow eyes.

"Hmmm," he thought. What should I do?"

Then he had an idea - a big monster truck to run over the city! He built a monster truck and called it Haunted Horizon because it was so big and scary.

One day when Johnny was riding his bike with Luciana, the gigantic monster truck interrupted their play. It ran over the trees, the grass, and the sidewalk.

"Duck!" cried Luciana as the monster truck approached them. The monster truck turned and started running over the playground. Johnny and Luciana flew up and distracted it, while Diego and Brian started attacking it from behind.

The monster truck stopped, and Prince Polo stepped out.

"Who are you?" asked Luciana.

"I am Prince Polo, son of the Evil King! You have destroyed my father, so now I will destroy your friend!"

He pushed a button. A giant air-breathing shark came out of the monster truck. Then out-stepped Brian with his hands tied behind his back.

"Wasn't he here just a minute ago?" asked Diego.

They all looked down. A robot that looked like Brian was there lying on the ground.

"Help!" cried the real Brian.

"He was a robot the whole time!" said Luciana.

They zipped off the ground and flew toward Brian.

"Oh no you don't!" screamed the prince.

He pressed a red button on the remote control he was holding. A robot hand shot out of the monster truck and pulled Brian and the shark back into the truck. The evil prince hopped into the truck and sped away.

"After them!" cried Johnny.

Johnny and the others flew off behind the monster truck. Suddenly, it disappeared.

"What happened?" asked Johnny.

"Where did it go?" asked Diego.

They all noticed that Luciana was chewing on something.

"Are you chewing bubblegum?" asked Diego

"No," said Luciana.

Everybody stared at her. There was a long silence. Then finally she said, "I'm chewing on rosemary."

"Rosemary?" shouted the others, and they started laughing.

"Magical rosemary," responded Luciana. "It takes you anywhere you want to go."

"Can we have a piece?" they asked.

"Sure!" said Luciana. She dropped a bit of rosemary in each of their hands.

Everybody popped it into their mouths and started chewing.

In an instant, a portal came out of nowhere. It started spinning 'round and 'round. They all hopped into the portal, and one minute later found themselves standing in the middle of the black and white world where the evil prince lived. When they got there, they all glanced up at the tall, creepy skyscraper looming above the kingdom.

"Guys, remember how the fox said the only way to get their color back was to find the key and unlock the magical cage?"

Everybody nodded.

"We have to find the key, otherwise they'll never be able to get their color back, and we may never see Brian again," explained Johnny.

"Guys! Look at that!" shouted Diego, pointing at the sky.

There, dangling from a string, was a tiny golden key. It was dangling from the roof of the skyscraper.

"I'll get it," said Diego, as he zoomed upward. When he was halfway there, he suddenly stopped and flew back to the ground.

"Guys, I can't get to it," said Diego. "There was a sign that read 'Only one superhero is allowed to fly up and take this key'. Immediately, I knew it wasn't me. I found this riddle right underneath it. I decided to take it back with me so we could figure out who is allowed to take the key."

Diego slowly read the riddle out loud.

"The superhero is a girl. She has blonde hair. She chews on rosemary to get around. The first letter of her first name begins with an "L". She is very smart and knows all the answers to her friends' questions. Her last name begins with the letter "P". She is very kind and sweet."

Everybody thought for a minute.

"Guys, It's me!" shouted Luciana.

"I don't think it's you," said Johnny.

"Prove it," replied Diego.

"Well, first of all, I am a girl," said Luciana. "Second of all, I have blonde hair. Third of all, I chew on rosemary to get around. Fourth of all, my name is Luciana. Fifth of all, I am very smart and I always answer your questions. Sixth of all, my last name is Parkenar. Seventh of all, I am very kind and sweet to you guys."

"Well, it's worth a try," said Johnny.

Luciana started flying upward. Finally, she reached the top, untied the golden key from the string, and flew back down to the ground.

"Good job Luciana!" said Diego when she reached the ground.

"Thanks guys!" said Luciana. "It was pretty easy."

They started walking down the path. They saw a pretty little lady come towards them. She was dressed in a black dress, wore black ear rings, and black shoes. Her hair was short and black.

"Excuse me, do you know where the magical cage is?" asked Johnny.

The lady pointed toward the center of the kingdom.

"Thank you," said Johnny as he walked down the path in its direction.

Minutes later, they all were standing in front of a big metal cage.

The cage was golden. In the center of it was a golden lock floating in the air. Johnny stepped inside of the cage and unlocked the lock. Suddenly, the ground began to shake. All of the black sidewalks and streets returned to their normal colors. All the buildings, people, cars and plants returned to their normal colors. All of the birds singing in the trees and all of the other animals changed back to their normal colors. The sky turned to a light blue. The clouds turned white.

As Johnny stepped outside of the cage, Luciana and Diego rushed over to him.

"Way to go, Johnny, we did it!" shouted Luciana.

Johnny beamed with pride.

CHAPTER SIX

THE PLAN

Johnny woke up the next morning. He thought he heard a commotion in the hallway outside the apartment. As he put his shoes on, his mother suddenly peeked out of her bedroom door.

"Johnny," she asked. "You should be at school. Where are you going?"

"I'm going to take a quick walk down the hallway," replied Johnny.

As he walked down the apartment building hallway, Johnny was surprised to see Luciana, Diego, and Brian tied up around a pole. He quickly hid behind a door and peeked out. He saw the evil prince approaching them with a smug look on his face.

"You brought color back to my kingdom. For revenge, I am going to destroy you and your friends," snickered the evil prince. He whistled four times and a shark appeared right in front of them with his mouth opened wide, ready to bite.

"Heeelp!" cried Diego, Luciana, and Brian at the same time.

"No!" shouted Johnny as he dashed out from behind the door and flew right at the greedy shark. "I'm not letting you eat any of my friends." He flew in circles around the shark to make him dizzy.

"Oh no you don't," cried the evil prince, as he took out a harpoon gun.

"Oh no you don't either!" shouted Johnny as he pulled out a piece of rosemary that Luciana had given him.

"Ha! What's a piece of rosemary going to do to me?" said the prince. "You destroyed my father, so I am going to destroy you!"

Johnny popped the piece of rosemary into his mouth and began to chew it. A portal appeared right in front of him. He leaped into the portal. He appeared on the roof of the tallest skyscraper in the dark world. He started searching through boxes and looking for supplies to help his friends. He found a long piece of rope, a fire alarm, a rope ladder, and a big rock. He quickly spit out his first piece of rosemary, took out a second piece, and started chewing.

Soon, he was inside the ceiling right above where his friends were tied up. He opened a tile from the ceiling, and looked down to see what was happening. The evil prince was sending off his guards to go find Johnny.

Johnny looped the rope around the big rock, tied the rope around his waist, and set aside the rope ladder. Then finally he pressed the fire alarm.

"WHEEEO WHEEEO WHEEEO WHEEO," went the fire alarm.

"See you later!" shouted the evil prince at the three teenagers.

The evil prince disappeared, and the guards disappeared one by one behind him.

"Help!" cried Luciana.

Then Johnny jumped out from the open ceiling tile and landed right behind them. He quickly untied the ropes that the evil prince had tied around them.

"Hold on, guys!" said Johnny as he climbed back up the rope through the open ceiling tile.

When he got back inside the ceiling, he threw down the rope ladder and said, "Guys, climb up the rope ladder!"

The three teenagers climbed up the rope ladder. When they reached inside the ceiling, he pulled up the rope ladder and closed the ceiling tile.

"Whew! That was a close one!" said Brian.

"It wasn't a close one. We are still in danger," said Luciana. "This place is about to blow up!"

"Well actually," said Johnny as he turned off the fire alarm. "I set the fire alarm."

"Really dude?" said Diego. "Why would you do that?"

"To distract the prince," explained Johnny as he untied the knot of the rope around his waist.

"So now what?" asked Diego. "Are we going to leave the supplies here and go back to school?"

"No." said Johnny. "We're going after that prince!"

CHAPTER SEVEN

THE HARDWORKING ROBOTS

"But how are we going to catch up with them?" asked Diego.

"Rosemary, of course!" said Luciana

Everybody took a piece of rosemary from Luciana, popped it into their mouths and began chewing. The portal opened, and seconds later they found themselves standing in front of the skyscraper again.

"Do you hear that?" asked Brian.

"Hear what?" asked Diego.

"Just listen hard, and you'll hear," replied Brian.

Suddenly, there were noises coming from the top of the skyscraper. Everybody flew to the top of the skyscraper and peeked into the top window. Everything in there was totally black. The prince was ordering robots to make bombs!

"Hurry up, you silly robots!" screamed the prince.

"We are trying, master, we are trying!" exclaimed the robots as they worked.

Suddenly, Diego pointed at the white crystal ball sitting on the prince's black table in front of his throne. The white crystal ball was showing Brian, Diego, Luciana, and Johnny watching the prince.

"Yeah, we should leave before we get caught," said Luciana.

Suddenly, the prince glanced up at his white crystal ball, and looked out the window that the kids were peeking into.

"Run!" exclaimed Diego.

Luciana gave each of them a piece of rosemary. Everybody started chewing. Suddenly, Johnny found himself on his living room couch.

Johnny began questioning himself. Would they be able to save the day and win the battle? What if they didn't survive? Would he let his mom down by letting the evil prince win? Johnny was so deep in thought that he didn't hear his mom calling.

"Johnny, dinner's ready!" she called.

"Oh, right," said Johnny as he jumped up from the couch.

For dinner, they were having salad, grilled chicken, and garlic mashed potatoes. Johnny ate all of his dinner, brushed his teeth, put on his pajamas and went to bed. Johnny stared at the starry sky still deep in thought. Then he said to himself, "Will I survive the battle?" Johnny closed his eyes and fell fast asleep.

CHAPTER EIGHT

THE ATTACKING ARMY OF GUARDS

The next day, Johnny, Luciana, Diego and Brian were biking at the park. Suddenly, a black giant ship with red windows flew over the city. It stopped. It sent an anchor to the ground. Then the evil prince's guards came climbing down the rope of the anchor. They started tying up people with gags and ropes.

The evil prince climbed down the rope and pulled out a big gun-like thing and pointed it at the sun. The machine started shooting out dark clouds, blotting out the sun.

"Wha ha haaaa! I have blocked the sun. Now soon the earth will be MINE!" yelled the evil prince.

"Follow me, guys. I know a way to trap that prince," said Johnny.

"This way," said Johnny as he flew up inside the ship.

Up there they began fighting the guards with their powers. When all the guards were defeated, they steered the ship toward the pitch-black sky. Higher and higher they went, till the ship reached space.

"Now we'll leave the ship here so the prince is trapped back on earth." said Johnny. "Let's head back to earth."

"How are we going to do that?" Asked Diego.

Johnny pulled out a chunk of rosemary out of his pocket.

"Hey, where did you get that from?" asked Brian.

"Luciana gave it to me while we were at the park," replied Johnny.

He put a little bit of rosemary into everybody's hand. Everybody began to chew.

Moments later they found themselves behind a bush in the park. Johnny told them his plan.

"Sounds like a good plan!" they all said.

Johnny sneaked up behind the prince and silently pulled the gun out of his back pocket.

Johnny pointed the gun toward the sky and pressed a button that said "sun".

Suddenly the clouds departed and the sun shone brightly in the sky.

The prince whirled around.

"You!!" he shrieked, pointing a finger at Johnny.

"Arrest him, guards!"

"If you are going to arrest him, you will have to go through us first!" Said a voice behind him. The prince turned around again, and was surprised to see Luciana, Diego, and Brian pointing fingers at him.

"Arrest them, too!" he snarled.

"Where are you going to lock us up? Didn't you notice that your ship is gone?" asked Johnny.

The prince fell to his knees, clawed his hands, and screamed "Nooooooo!"

The police arrived and forced him into a police car.

"Thanks for finding him. We also caught all the guards," said the police.

Johnny, Luciana, Brian and Diego helped untie all of the people that the prince and his guards had tied up.

That night Johnny fell asleep right away, knowing that the prince was safely behind bars.

CHAPTER NINE

PICKING OUT COSTUMES

The next day Luciana, Johnny, Diego and Brian were at Superhero Training in the auditorium. The trainers were passing out awards. When the awards were done, a man stood up and said, "Diego, Luciana, Brian and Johnny, please step onstage."

They got up and walked onto the stage.

"Even though you four are underage, we have made an exception. You have officially graduated from Superhero Training."

Then Dr. Morgan said, "And now for your costumes."

They followed Dr. Morgan to a big room with lots of mannequins wearing super hero costumes.

"So, what do you want?" asked Dr. Morgan.

Everybody wandered around the room searching for the best costume.

Luciana came out of a clothes rack with a sparkly, turquoise gown.

Johnny found a blue jumpsuit. Diego found a red fire proof suit. Brian found a yellow suit with a lightning bolt on it.

When Johnny got home, he couldn't wait to eat dinner.

CHAPTER TEN

THE NEXT MISSION

Johnny's tummy was rumbling so loud, that it shook the whole apartment.

Johnny's mom said, "Johnny, you are sooo hungry," as she put down garlic mashed potatoes.

"Mom, what's for dinner?" asked Johnny.

"Garlic mashed potatoes, cooked broccoli, and steak," she replied.

Johnny ate his dinner and went right to bed. That night Johnny fell fast asleep, dreaming of saving the world.

The next day, Johnny met up with the others at the playground.

"So, what do you want your superhero names to be?" he asked them.

"Burning Bro," replied Diego.

"Agua Girl," said Luciana.

"Electroplate," said Brian, coolly.

"I'll be Ice Boy," said Johnny.

Suddenly, the playground equipment began to shake. A rumbling noise came from behind them. As they spun around, they saw a big army of slimy monsters heading their way. Everybody looked at each other. They all knew it was time for their next mission.

TO BE CONTINUED…

About the Author

A. Marino is 8 years old. She lives in Maryland with her mom, dad, and younger brother. She published her first picture book, *Berry Poppins and Emily*, at age 5. She also wrote and illustrated *Kindergarten, Here We Come, Berry Poppins and Emily and the First Day of Christmas*, and *Berry Poppins and Emily and Valentine's Day*. She likes superheroes, dancing, and loves to read and write stories. This is her first chapter book.